MW01595039

Greater Than Gold

Poems That Celebrate a Relationship with God

Frances Gregory Pasch

GREATER THAN GOLD: POEMS THAT CELEBRATE A
RELATIONSHIP WITH GOD BY FRANCES GREGORY PASCH

Published by Lightning Editing Services
ISBN: 9798559528007
Copyright © 2020 by Frances Gregory Pasch
Cover design by M. H. Pasindu Lakshan
Interior design by Uplift Editing
Chapter title scroll by Gordon Johnson from Pixabay.com
Poem scroll by Rebecca Read from Pixabay.com
Author photograph by Scott Richard

Available in print from amazon.com.

For more information on this book and the author, visit
www.francesgregorypasch.com

All Scripture quotations, unless otherwise indicated, are taken from the
Holy Bible, New International Version®, NIV.® Copyright ©1973, 1978,
1984 by International Bible Society.® Used by permission. All rights
reserved worldwide.

Scriptures marked ESV are taken from The Holy Bible, English
Standard Version® (ESV®), copyright © 2001 by Crossway, a
publishing ministry of Good News Publishers. Used by permission. All
rights reserved.

Printed in the United States of America

Praise for *Greater Than Gold*
Poems That Celebrate a Relationship with God

As always, beautiful reflections of life! Fran writes with eyes that 'see' beyond this world, her poetry giving me glimpses of God's ways and works in everyday life. I love her sensitivity to the Spirit's voice. Let these lines lift your heart to God's Presence and help you to find words of praise and thanksgiving as you read them. The joy of the Lord shines through each page.

Rev. Jerry Scott
Senior Pastor, Faith Discovery Church

Frances Gregory Pasch invites readers to celebrate with joy and thanksgiving, the richness—the "pure gold"—of God's love to us in Jesus Christ. A veritable poetry party not to be missed!

Helene Clare Kuoni
Author, *A Walk in the Sunshine*
and *Her Pen for His Glory*
Former Editorial Assistant for *The Secret Place*
Elder, Grace Church Bethlehem, Bethlehem, PA

Fran's poems are such a blessing and inspiration! Not only do they clearly explain the gospel of Jesus Christ, they also offer words of wisdom for readers and reveal some of her personal struggles as she faithfully lives and writes for her Savior. Readers will be inspired, challenged, and blessed.

Kathleen Hayes
Freelance Editor
Former Senior Editor of *The Secret Place*

In her latest collection of inspired poetry, Fran Pasch offers a glimpse of her intimate relationship with God and how we, too, can enjoy Him.

Woven into this treasure of poems are heartfelt prayers and confessions, messages from the Lord, personal testimony, godly advice, and challenges on how to abide in Christ.

You will be blessed and encouraged by each verse she has so lovingly written!

Rev. Annalee Davis
Author, Speaker, Retired Pastor

Through the gift of lyrical verse, Frances encourages the reader to walk with the Lord and talk with the Lord at all times and in all ways.

Her words are simple, yet powerful messages that work to eradicate doubt and fear in order to achieve perfect peace in everyday living.

Pam Giordano
Author, *Promises to Keep*

In *Greater Than Gold*, Fran takes us on a journey through a life of faith. Her reflections in the midst of doubt show hope and growth. This causes us to confront our own relationship with Christ.

Her transparent conversations with God, which mirror our own concerns, assure us of His love and nearness as we manage each new day. This book of poetry will delight and challenge.

Elona Logan Harkins, CPRW
Freelance Writer and Blogger of Breakseverychain.com

In reading about Fran's relationship with God, we see that all of us can be, in some way, partakers of her journey. Fran shows us that it is possible to know and celebrate God personally, in a pure intimacy that is available nowhere else, yet open to anyone who will put their trust in Him. Her poems refresh our spirits as she helps us to see what is truly important and invites us to join her in her daily walk with the One who knows us best yet loves us deeply. I believe it is her prayer that you will find rest in Him.

Deborah Gatz
Member of Hawk Pointe Writers' Group,
Asst. Women's Bible Teacher
First Baptist Church, Phillipsburg, NJ

Like water poured out on a parched soul, Fran's poetic voice satisfies. Opening up the heart with simple phrases, she has mastered the inner art of healing with words. Words of encouragement, healing, and triumph fill the pages. *Greater Than Gold* is a thoughtful collection of life's verses—written by the author, inspired by God.

Sally Puleo
Author, Nurse, Assemblies of God Missionary

I dedicate this book to my Lord and Savior,
Jesus Christ.

It is He who gifted me
with the ability to write poetry
after I surrendered my life to Him.

Table of Contents

Conversations with God

Look to the Lord

Freedom in Christ

God Is Everywhere

Questions for Meditation

The Lord, My Helper

Words Are Powerful

God's Christmas Gift

Easter Blessings

Foreword

The rhythm of poetry caresses our spirit unlike anything else, lifting us up with promise and assurance. No matter what the day brings, we can find rest in the melody of poetry. For it's there we find words to soothe our weary minds, and words that inexplicably speak into all lives. That's the mystery of Verse and the mystery of God.

In *Greater Than Gold: Poems That Celebrate a Relationship with God,* Fran delivers nuggets of truth that draw us back into harmony with our Creator, compelling us to slow down and reflect on the Source of life, rather than the often chaotic circumstances.

Fran uses simple words of hope to echo the simple message of the gospel. During complex times, plain truth is a welcome change. I'm blessed to call her a mentor and friend.

> In an age of discontent,
>> Where toxic banters flow,
>>> A wonderful respite awaits,
>>>> In words that ebb and flow.
> Refreshing us to life again,
>> By bringing forth this truth,
>>> That Jesus is our faithful friend,
>>>> Our peace, our hope, our youth.

May you enjoy this book of poetry as you reflect on God's precious gift of life.

Jewell Utt
Author and Inspirational Speaker
Consider the Birds: Reflections to Make You Soar
www.jewellutt.com

Acknowledgments

A special thank-you to my husband, Jim. He has been my best encourager and supporter. I am extremely grateful to have him in my life.

Thanks to our five sons: Jimmy, Glenn, Brian, Scott, and Stephen. Each of them has blessed us in so many ways.

Thanks also to our nine grandchildren: April, Alexandra, Rebecca, Connor, Faith, Stephen, William, Alexander, and Dillon. Each of them holds a special place in our hearts.

I am grateful to all the ladies who have attended my writers' critique group since I launched it in 1991. Thank you for your encouragement, advice, and friendship. It's exciting to see the progress you each have achieved.

A special thank-you to my writer friend, Denise Loock, who edited this book and helped me put it together.

Life Is a Journey

Think of life as a journey
That follows the path where God leads.
There's no need for us to be anxious
For He'll provide all of our needs.

He pledges to be there beside us
In good times and those that are bad.
He promises peace and contentment
And He'll dry our tears when we're sad.

How blessed we are as God's children
With a Father so faithful and kind,
Who promises never to leave us
Who gives us true peace of mind.

Introduction

Although I have believed in God since I was young, I never realized I could have a personal relationship with Him until I was much older.

In 1983, at the age of 50, I invited Jesus to be my Lord and Savior. When I began reading the Bible and learned more about Him, my life became an action-packed journey, with my family and with my God-given gift of writing poems and devotions. Despite ups and downs, my faith continues to grow each day.

Greater Than Gold: Poems That Celebrate a Relationship with God emphasizes the value of my personal relationship with Jesus. The sectional themes reflect the ways I connect with Him during my daily devotional time.

I pray that the poems in this book will encourage you to draw closer to God.

Conversations with God

*Trust in the Lord with all your heart
and lean not on your own understanding;
in all your ways acknowledge him,
and he will make your paths straight.*

Proverbs 3:5–6

Believing Is a Must

Before I knew You, Jesus,
I'd worry and I'd fret.
Each time bad news came my way,
I'd really get upset.

Now I try to analyze
The news that I receive;
I look beyond the surface
So I will not be deceived.

I have learned, dear Jesus,
At times I must bear pain.
I also know there will be times
That You will not explain.

I'm learning to accept what comes…
In You alone I trust,
For if I'm to be faithful…
Believing is a must!

Heavenly Treasures

Dear Jesus, You have shown me
By Your guidance and Your love,
The things that I must strive for
Are the things that are above.

They're the only things that matter.
They're the only things of worth.
For when I die I cannot take
My treasures stored on earth.

So help me, Lord, to concentrate
On ways to love and share.
Show me where I'm needed.
Let others know I care.

Don't let the devil fill my mind
With thoughts of fear and dread.
Just let me feed upon Your Word
And trust in You instead.

3

Thank You, God

Thank You, God,
For using the everyday things
I experience
To help others.

I pray that the lessons
I have learned
Will spare them pain.

Let me share with others
How walking with You
Has made my path easier,
My way brighter,
And each new day more joyful.

Frances Gregory Pasch

I Know I Will Achieve

I know I'm where You want me, Lord,
That's why I do believe
The plans You have in mind for me
I truly will achieve.

Because You are in charge of
All the things I have to do,
I know I have Your promise
That You will see me through.

So when I face a mountain
That seems too high to climb
With You beside me every step
I'll scale it in Your time.

I Must Not Leave You Behind

When I awake in the morning, God,
You're the first One on my mind.
Each place I go I take You
I must not leave You behind.

I ask Your help with decisions
We chat throughout the day,
With You by my side every moment
I'm less apt to go astray.

The world tries to change my focus,
It vies for attention and time,
But if I want to stay on track
I must not leave You behind.

Frances Gregory Pasch

Forgive Me, Lord

When the earth with its temptations
Tries to get my life off track,
And I spend time doing worldly things
And sometimes turn my back…

Forgive me.

When I try to work things my own way
Instead of trusting You,
When I think I have the answers
Yet they seldom see me through…

Forgive me.

When I wrestle with anxiety
And get uptight inside,
And continually rely on me
And bathe myself in pride…

Forgive me.

Help me, Lord, to lean on You,
Provide the strength I need.
For in Your power and with Your grace
I know I can succeed.

One of Those Days

Today I'm overwhelmed, Lord…
Not by big things,
Just those everyday chores.

You know…
Cooking and cleaning,
Washing and ironing,
Shopping and chauffeuring—
There's never an end.

I need an extra dose
Of Your Holy Spirit
To refresh me.

Renew my strength,
So that I may serve You better.

Godly Advice

On days when things get hectic, Lord,
And my head is spinning around,
You take me by the shoulders
And You gently sit me down.

You whisper, "Do not panic
Relax and stop a while…
Fatigue causes tension
And robs you of your smile.

"Put everything in order,
Get your priorities straight…
Forget unneeded details,
On key things concentrate.

"You don't have to impress Me,
It's not how much you do,
It's the way in which you do things…
Just keep My will in view.

"For whatever you accomplish
It's not for you, but Me.
If you put Me first, you'll triumph
And dwell with Me eternally."

Little Things

God, with You in my life,
An ordinary day often becomes
A momentous one.

Little things take on new meanings.
They happen when I least expect them.
A note, a call, an e-mail…
Just at the right time.
And that's what makes them special.

How blessed I am that I can
Always count on You
To do what's best for me.

Frances Gregory Pasch

Nighttime Visits

Thank You, Lord, for our nighttime visits
When the only noise is the ticking of the clock.

I can hear Your voice much clearer now—
Not audibly, but Your thoughts penetrate
Deeply in the darkness.

Though my body craves sleep,
This time with You is more important.

In the daytime I do spend time with You,
But so often the world drowns You out.
So in the middle of the night Your voice is precious.

I know You enjoy spending time with me
As much as I enjoy spending time with You.

Look to the Lord

*Come near to God
and he will come near to you.*

James 4:8

A Good Start

When I get up in the morning
I offer Jesus my day.
I ask for His blessing and guidance
And pray from His path not to stray.

I get a nice feeling inside me
Just knowing that He always cares;
Regardless of what I am doing,
My joys and my sorrows He shares.

My days are not always easy;
Some pain I know I must bear.
Still everything seems so much easier,
Just knowing that Jesus is there.

Frances Gregory Pasch

Just Chat with Him

You need not pray down on your knees,
It can be underneath the trees,
Or in the house, or in a bank,
In a grocery line or filling your tank.

No formal words does God require.
Just chat with Him—that's His desire.
It can be in the day or night.
Any time will be all right.

What matters most is don't forget
And get so busy that you let
Things block Him out of all you do,
For He would not do that to you.

He wants to be your closest friend.
On Him alone you can depend.

The Right View

Sometimes the grass looks greener
In someone else's life.
It seems their days run smoother…
There's much less stress and strife.

Their kids behave much better
Their money provides more.
Their future seems much brighter…
They have blessings by the score.

Yet when I stop to ponder
All that God has done for me,
I need to stop comparing
And get down on my knees.

For I am where He wants me.
There's a reason for His plans.
And if I want His best for me,
I'll leave things in His hands.

16

Frances Gregory Pasch

Look to Him

If life seems overwhelming
And you feel your future's dim,
Don't become discouraged...

Look to Him.

If your children are backsliding
And recovery seems quite slim,
Don't agonize or worry...

Look to Him.

If you think your job's protected
But your company starts to trim,
Don't think the worst or panic...

Look to Him.

If all the heinous crimes on earth
Depict your future grim,
Remember God is still in charge...

Look to Him.

Don't let the devil crush your hope,
Stand strong and sing a hymn.
Nothing pleases our God more
Than when we look to Him.

Waiting

Waiting for answers
Is part of God's plan
To strengthen our faith
As we rest in His hands.

We don't like to wait,
We want answers now.
We know He could grant them
He surely knows how.

Yet He puts us on hold
Doesn't give us a reason
For His plans yield fruit
In His perfect season.

So while we are waiting
We stretch and we grow
For His timing is perfect,
Not fast or too slow.

Learning to Wait

Lord, I'm learning
That when You don't answer
My prayers right away,
There's a good reason.

Perhaps I need to change first,
Perhaps I need to grow more,
Perhaps I can't handle the outcome.

I'm learning that You are able
To reveal the reason for Your delays,
But You may not always do that.

I'm learning that Your ways
Are always better than mine,
That You are able to bless me
Abundantly more than I ever dreamed.

Lord, I'm learning.

If I Never Stop to Listen

I cannot hear You, Jesus,
If I run around all day
And never stop to listen
To the words You want to say.

I need You on my schedule
As the most important thing…
Make You first each day I waken
Praise You as my Lord and King.

If I give You my attention
Heed the words You have to say…
Remind myself You love me
Then I'll enjoy each day.

Frances Gregory Pasch

Will Your Treasures Last?

Are you running on empty?
Are you walking too fast?
Accomplishing things
That you know will not last?

Are you storing up treasures
Here on the earth...
Though you know in your heart
They have no lasting worth?

Why not change directions?
Seek God and His plan...
When you focus on Him
He'll take hold of your hand.

He wants to direct you
There's no better Guide...
Plus His Holy Spirit
Will be at your side.

Your pace will be slower
You might not walk fast...
But the treasures you're storing
Are those that will last.

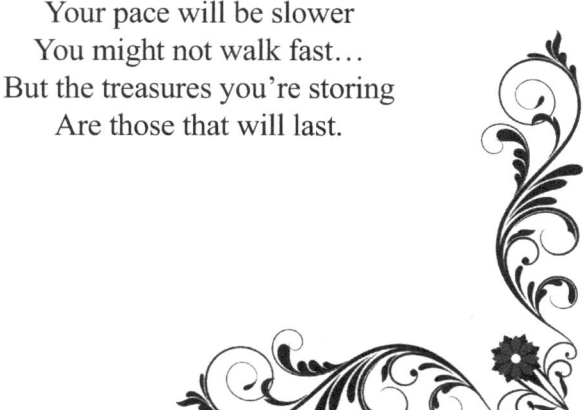

Freedom in Christ

Therefore, if anyone is in Christ,
he is a new creation.
The old has passed away;
Behold, the new has come.

2 Corinthians 5:17 (ESV)

In Christ Alone Is Salvation

The world's in a state of confusion
But we can have peace every day.
The key is believing that Jesus
Is the Truth, the Life, and the Way.

In Him alone is salvation.
He came so we can be free.
In Him there's no condemnation.
He shed blood for you and for me.

He assures us of living forever
With Him in heaven above.
We're blessed to call Him our Savior.
We're doubly blessed by His love.

No Greater Deal

Are you afraid of dying?
Do you know your destiny?
Do you have an anxious feeling
About your security?

Do you wonder where you're headed?
Do you think that heaven's real?
Have you heard about salvation?
There is no greater deal.

It's promised in the Bible...
An eternal guarantee.
Nothing down, was paid in full
By Christ on Calvary.

You can say the words in private
Or when you're in a crowd.
You can say them very softly
Or boldly speak them loud.

Just tell the Lord you're sorry...
Repent of all your sin.
Believe that He has paved the way...
Then He will enter in.

The Key to Freedom

Driving down the highway
Sandwiched in by two trucks,
I feel fearless.

I used to be afraid
Of driving distances
Of riding in the middle lane
Of going places alone.

But God freed me
When I handed Him
The keys to my life.

Frances Gregory Pasch

Remind Me, Lord

You set me free,
Yet sometimes I forget
The freedom I possess.

When I let Satan
Immobilize me
By allowing old habits
To resurface,

When I struggle
In my own strength
Instead of walking
In Your power,

Remind me, Lord,
That Your yoke is easy
And Your burden is light.

Remind me, Lord,
That You will never leave me.
It is I who go astray.

The Key to Victory

More of You and less of me
That's the key to victory!

I tried to make it on my own
By the works that I had sown
But now I know it's by Your grace
That I shall see You face to face.

It's by Your death on Calvary
That You, My Lord, have set me free.

You rose again so I can too;
I'll spend eternity with You.
No greater gift can I receive…
All I must do is just believe.

Frances Gregory Pasch

You'll Always Be a Child of God

You'll always be a Child of God
Regardless of your age,
And He'll always be your Father,
Always faithful, always sage.

You can surely trust His judgment
For He knows what's best for you;
Your ideas and His may differ
But it's His will you must do.

For when you struggle on your own
Planning things your way,
You leave Him in the background,
And you'll surely go astray.

So stop and take a minute;
Listen carefully to His voice.
He will calm your indecision,
And help you make each choice.

God Is Everywhere

For the eyes of the Lord
range throughout the earth
to strengthen those
whose hearts are fully committed to him.

2 Chronicles 16:9

God's Love

God's love has no boundaries
It's flowing everywhere…
He has enough for everyone
And even some to spare.

So take a heaping handful
And give some out each day…
Speak it by your actions
And with the words you say.

As you share His love with others
He'll make it multiply…
For God's love has no boundaries
There's an infinite supply.

Frances Gregory Pasch

God's Everyday Blessings

He's the smile on a face…
A note in the mail.
The breeze on the ocean
That propels a sail.

Food in the pantry…
Wood on the fire.
Shoes on our feet…
Words that inspire.

Let's not get so busy
That we miss all His signs…
They're His way of blessing
Both your days and mine.

I See You, Lord

I see You in the flowers.
I hear You in the trees.
I feel Your awesome presence
In the cool and gentle breeze.

I see You in the smile
Of a peaceful, joyful face.
I feel that You are with me,
As I bow my head for grace.

Help me, Lord, to rest in You
And treasure all my days,
For if I get too busy,
I'll miss Your choice bouquets.

Awesome

I hear You in the silence.
I hear You in the storm.
I hear You in the baby's cry.
I see You in the dawn.

I feel Your peace each morning
And all throughout the day.
I feel Your peace at bedtime
And every time I pray.

Your awesomeness surrounds me
In everything I do.
How blessed I am to have a God
As wonderful as You.

Comforting Counselor

Comforting Counselor
Defender Divine...
Righteous Rewarder
Victorious Vine.

Barrier Breaker
True Prince of Peace...
Fairest Forgiver
Whose love will not cease.

Protector, Provider
Prophet and Priest...
Bridegroom and Brother
Friend of the Least.

Rock and Redeemer
Soon-Coming King...
Shepherd and Savior
Our Everything!

Frances Gregory Pasch

My Best Friend

Jesus is more than my Savior
He's also my very best friend.
He's here whenever I need Him.
On Him I can always depend.

He wakes me every morning
He's with me all through the day,
And when I'm ready to go to bed
Beside me all night He will stay.

I have no other friend like Him.
He answers whenever I call.
He only wants what's best for me.
He picks me up each time I fall.

And although He is my best friend
He can be your best friend too,
For His love has no boundaries
He has lots left just for you.

So stop and take a minute;
Welcome Him into your heart.
You'll have a wonderful feeling
That only His peace can impart.

Questions for Meditation

May the words of my mouth
and the meditation of my heart
be pleasing in your sight,
O Lord, my Rock and my Redeemer.

Psalm 19:14

Why, Lord?

Why do we only call You
When in trouble or in pain?
When things are going our way
There's no reason to complain.

But as soon as there is conflict,
And we don't know what to do,
We lift our eyes and raise our voice
And plead our case with You.

Why is it that we keep in touch
Just when we need Your help?
Why do we try continuously
To do things by ourselves?

Why don't we come to recognize
That Your way is the best;
That if we learn to lean on You
Our lives will be at rest.

Frances Gregory Pasch

Where Are You Headed?

Do you sometimes stop and wonder
Where the path you're following leads?
Does it have a destination?
Does it really meet your needs?

Do you know where you are headed
Or do you trudge along,
Not knowing where it all will end
Or if you're right or wrong?

Then, stop and take a minute
Before it is too late.
Reassess the life you're living;
Don't leave anything to fate.

For there is only one path
With salvation as its reward…
It's the winding road to heaven,
And your Savior, Christ our Lord.

Why Do We Look Afar?

Why is it that we look afar
For what is really near?
We wish for things we think we need,
When, actually, they're right here.

Our nature is a wishful one;
We're often discontent.
We're waiting for the future,
While we're missing the present.

Perhaps we should take stock today
Of what we have right now,
And enjoy the many blessings
With which we've been endowed.

Why plan for tomorrow
Over which we've no control?
Let's enjoy today, while it is here
And calm our anxious souls.

Frances Gregory Pasch

Do You Wonder?

Sometimes I sit and ponder
About the years gone by.
I think about what I have done
And often question why.

Perhaps if I knew way back then
The things that I know now,
I may have changed a thing or two,
But I did what I knew how.

It doesn't pay to speculate
On what could have happened if…
For going back just wastes today
And makes my future drift.

So now I'm taking each new day,
Walking straight and tall,
For if I don't step out in faith,
I'll get nowhere at all.

How Will I React?

When alarming news invades my life
My reaction is concern.
I wonder why it's happening
Yet through the years I've learned

That God knows what is happening
And on Him I can always count
To quiet my fears and worries
So above them I can mount.

For if I choose to rest in Him
Instead of relying on me,
I will not feel anxious.
I'll feel serenity.

Frances Gregory Pasch

What If?

A knock on the door…
"Too busy!" I say.
I'll just keep on working
Then they'll go away.

Can't stop what I'm doing…
No time to chat.
Someday in the future
I'll take time for that.

Talking wastes time…
Must get my work done.
No time to visit …
Must be on the run.

I can't be like Mary…
And sit at Christ's feet.
I must clean the house,
Bake the bread, cook the meat.

But Jesus says, "Martha,
What if today
It was I who was knocking
And you turned Me away?"

The Lord, My Helper

I lift up my eyes to the hills—
where does my help come from?
My help comes from the Lord,
the Maker of heaven and earth.

Psalm 121:1–2

The Master Conductor

Instead of following Your lead, Lord,
I often exhaust myself
Trying to orchestrate my own life.

How blessed I am
That You love me enough
To direct my steps,
To tune my spirit to Your will,
And keep me on key
As you are composing
The rest of my life's story.

Continue to remind me
That Your pauses are perfect,
Your tempo is right,
And I don't have to sing
Anyone else's song.
I only need to follow Your lead.

Frances Gregory Pasch

Guide Me, Lord

When I complain,
Set me straight.
When impatient,
Help me wait.

When too busy,
Slow me down.
When I'm cranky,
Erase my frown.

Guide the path
Where I'm to go.
Teach me all
That I must know.

Hold my hand
Along the way;
Don't let Satan
Lead me astray.

Let me live
For You alone;
When life's over,
Take me home.

A Slip of the Lip

I did it again, Lord,
Opened my mouth
At the wrong time...
Not once,
But three times.

Why did I have to say
"Comb your hair"?
Why wasn't I just happy
That he was going to church
With me?

Am I still worried about
What others think?
I thought I had
Overcome that.

In retrospect,
My heart
Was more disheveled
Than his hair.

Frances Gregory Pasch

The Right Perspective

Help me put things in perspective
Before I criticize.
Let me view the situation
From the other person's eyes.

For words come forth so easily,
Sometimes I blurt them out.
I speak fast, without thinking
What my words are all about.

Why is it I am quick to speak
And often fail to see,
The price my hasty words may have,
How harmful they can be?

Perhaps if I would think things through
Before I verbalize,
I soon would learn to overcome
My need to criticize.

It's You I Must Please

Lord, help me
To never compromise
The Gospel,

Remove my desire
To please everyone
At the expense
Of displeasing You.

Imprint Your Word
So deeply in my heart
That I will proclaim
The Good News
Unceasingly
With Holy Spirit boldness
For Your glory.

Frances Gregory Pasch

Help Me to Be Satisfied

Lord, don't let me be intimidated
By the accomplishments of others.
When I see their long list of credits,
I'm tempted to say
"I'll never be that good."

Instead, help me to concentrate
On my abilities.
Let me use them
The best way I can.

Instead of envying others,
Let me pray for them.
Let me be happy that You
Are using them for Your glory too.

Help me to be satisfied
With small beginnings,
Trusting You to open
Bigger doors
In Your perfect timing.

God's Measuring Stick

God, I tend to measure my life
By how much I do.

When I physically see
What I have accomplished,
I feel good about myself.

The world measures success
That way too…
It equates success
With high positions,
Material possessions,
And money.

How blessed I am, Lord,
That You measure my life
By things of eternal value.

Frances Gregory Pasch

Equip Me, Lord

Sometimes the valleys in my life
Loom larger than
My mountaintop experiences.
But often the valleys
Are of my own making.

I dwell on the past,
Wallow in self-pity,
Rehash my failures,
And exaggerate my problems.

I try to rest in You,
But it's not always easy.

Help me to listen to You,
Through Your Word,
Through my circumstances,
And through other believers.

Fill me with Your Holy Spirit
So I can walk in Your footsteps.

Then I will be equipped
To show others the way.

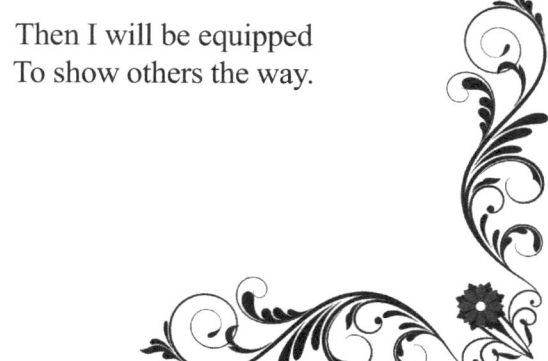

Words Are Powerful

Reckless words
pierce like a sword,
but the tongue of the wise
brings healing.

Proverbs 12:18

My Writing Aim

Polishing the perfect poem
Takes talent, thought, and time.
The words must have a message
Whether free verse or in rhyme.

I aim to touch the readers' hearts
With words they won't forget...
Instill a thought or soothe a hurt
But even better yet,

To turn a soul toward Jesus
Giving someone hope,
Offering encouragement...
An aid to help them cope

Frances Gregory Pasch

What Really Counts

Sometimes I think
That my words are too simple…
That they lack the flair
Of other writers' words.

But Jesus reminds me
That His words are simple too…
Straightforward
And right to the point.

When I look at my writing
From His perspective,
I realize
That it doesn't matter
How elaborate my words are.

What really counts
Is that Christ
Is glorified.

Final Draft

Lord, help me delete all the fluff
And any other useless stuff.
Help me get right to the point
Into the marrow and the joint.

Help my words to penetrate,
By being simple—not ornate.
Let my message ring out clear
So those who read will want to hear.

Your Word says that You rejoice
If just one sinner heeds Your voice.
Use me, Lord, in some small way…
That's my writing prayer today.

Frances Gregory Pasch

Don't Wait!

Ideas are so elusive
We need to write them down.
We think that we'll remember
But often we have found

That when we try to capture them
They are no longer there…
The special thoughts we treasured
Have vanished in the air.

So write them down the minute
They come into your mind—
Then you'll have a legacy
That you can leave behind.

Unspoken Love

Dad, you couldn't say "I love you"
But when I held your hand
And saw the way you looked at me
I came to understand

That in your heart you loved me
Though those words you could not say,
For your parents never said them,
They did not know the way.

They didn't show affection
Nor tell you how they cared,
That's why you couldn't say them...
Those words you never shared.

But I'm so glad before you died
I got the chance to feel
Your love in many other ways
And knew that it was real.

A Legacy of Words

Dad, today I clipped beautiful roses
From your garden.
Actually, it's my garden
Now that you're gone,
But you left your fingerprints in the soil
For me to remember you by.

The garden will never look
As nice as when you were alive.
You had a special knack
For making things grow.

I don't plant seeds in the ground
As you did,
But I do plant seeds in people's hearts
With the words I write.

I hope that after I'm gone
My poems and stories
Will leave my fingerprints
On those I leave behind.

Now!

Wasted minutes, wasted hours
Time that we cannot reclaim.
Help us, Lord, to keep our focus,
So we won't waste time again.

If we don't put words on paper
How will others get to hear?
Help us, Lord, to write Your message,
Help us make it very clear.

Show us how to use time wisely
Help us not procrastinate.
Help us tell the Gospel message
Now, before it is too late.

Frances Gregory Pasch

Words Change Lives

Sometimes we speak them hastily
And regret it.
Other times we remain silent
And wish we had spoken.

Words come in all sizes…
Many are small, yet dynamic.
Others are big
But of little importance.

We can change lives by what we say…
Either for good or for bad.
Our words can make people laugh
Or make them cry.

Words can build them up
Or bring them down…
Pull them closer or turn them away.

Whether written or spoken,
Rehearsed or spontaneous,
Words are powerful.
They are easy to come by,
But not easily forgotten.

A good reason to measure them out carefully.

God's Christmas Gift

*For God so loved the world
that he gave his one and only son,
that whoever believes in him
shall not perish
but have eternal life.*

John 3:16

Let's Not Forget

Amidst the hustle bustle
Of our busy world today…
Let's stop and take a minute
To thank the Lord and pray.

Let's not forget His precious gift,
The reason why He came…
Salvation is in Christ alone,
Not any other name.

From a baby in a manger
To the cross at Calvary…
Christ came to earth with us in mind
So He could set us free.

How blessed we are to have a God
Who wants us to receive…
Eternal life wrapped in His arms
It's ours, if we'll believe.

Frances Gregory Pasch

Jesus, Our Savior

In fulfillment of the Scriptures
Jesus came to earth,
Not as a man, but as a child,
His was a humble birth.

There were no crowds to greet Him,
No party or fanfare,
Just a simple setting,
He entered unaware.

But the reason for His coming
Is one that must be told…
He's the key to our salvation,
Prophesied from days of old.

He took on human nature
So He could bear our sin
Upon the cross, in place of us,
So new life could begin.

What greater gift could we receive
Than His abounding grace…
The promise that we'll one day share
His presence face to face!

Our Bridge Builder

A baby wrapped in swaddling clothes
Lying in a manger...
To some He is the Son of God
To others He's a stranger.

It's sad to think that all don't know
His true identity...
That He is both true God and man
Who came to set us free.

If only they would recognize
The power in His name...
It would change their lives forever
They'd never be the same.

For only He can bridge the gap
Left open by man's sin...
He alone will welcome us
The day we enter in.

Frances Gregory Pasch

No Room in the Inn

"No room in the inn," they heard the man say.
Discouraging news on a long weary day.
"Go to the stable, bed down in the hay;
That's the best I can do, if you'd like to stay."

Since Mary and Joseph were tired and worn
And needed a place for their child to be born,
They went to the place where the animals lay
And made a small bed for the babe out of hay.

Right before dawn, a cry could be heard…
A Savior was born—the True Living Word.
The awaited Redeemer, sent from above…
A gift from the Father, a true act of love.

Unless Jesus came, there would be no way
To enter heaven on our final day.
Let's open our hearts so we can receive
His free gift to all who choose to believe.

God's Gift to Us

Still cloaked in His divinity
Christ stepped into humanity.
Encompassed by virginity
He entered in simplicity.

There was no Christmas greenery
No pomp, nor fancy scenery.
Just boundless love for you and me...
Christ's destination—Calvary.

If we'll believe He set us free,
Christ promises that we will be
With Him for all eternity...
His priceless gift of victory.

Frances Gregory Pasch

What Will Your Focus Be?

When the holidays are over
And your tree is packed away
Will your presents or Christ's presence
Be the focus of each day?

Will Jesus be a special part
Of all you say and do?
Will you accept the gift of life
He freely offers you?

He came to earth to cleanse our sins
That's why He had to die.
We cannot earn salvation
No matter how we try.

He waits for us with open arms
What will your answer be?
If you'll say yes, He promises
Eternal security.

Easter Blessings

If you confess with your mouth.
"Jesus is Lord,"
and believe in your heart
that God raised him from the dead,
you will be saved.

Romans 10:9

As We Await Easter

As we await Easter,
Let us prepare our hearts
To welcome our Savior.

Let us thank Christ
For His gift of redemption.
Let us share with others
What He has done for us.

Let us contemplate with awe
The true meaning
Of Christ's death
And resurrection.

Frances Gregory Pasch

Christ Is Risen

Let's look beyond the Easter scene
Of colored eggs and jelly beans.
Let's set our eyes upon the Lord
And feast instead upon His Word.

Let's not forget that we'd be lost
Had Jesus not died on the cross.
He nailed our sins upon the tree
And rose again so we'd be free.

So let's sing out in jubilation;
Christ alone is our salvation.
Lord and Savior—Counselor, King,
Great Provider—our Everything.

He Set Us Free

"What shall I do with Jesus?"
Pilate asked the angry crowd.
"What crime has he committed
That you should scream so loud?"

They shouted, "Crucify Him!"
Pilate grudgingly gave in
But washed his hands because he knew
That Jesus hadn't sinned.

They stripped Him and they beat Him,
Pressed thorns into His head.
With no remorse or sorrow,
They stood at the cross and said,
"Save yourself if you're the king
And come down from the cross,"
Yet Jesus never said a word...
He came to save the lost.

He paid our debt, then rose again...
By grace He set us free.
If we'll believe and trust in Him,
We'll live eternally.

78

Frances Gregory Pasch

An Eternal Legacy

You could have come down from the cross
And spared Yourself great pain
For there was nothing stopping You…
Yet You chose to remain.

You knew that someone had to pay
The price for mankind's sin.
You knew that if You turned Your back
The Enemy would win.

Despite the people's jeering
And defaming of Your name,
You walked the road to Calvary
Enduring unjust shame.

You let them nail You to the cross
Without a word or sigh
So we could have eternal life…
In our place You would die.

The priceless legacy You left
Is filled with love and grace…
You promise that if we believe
We'll see You face to face.

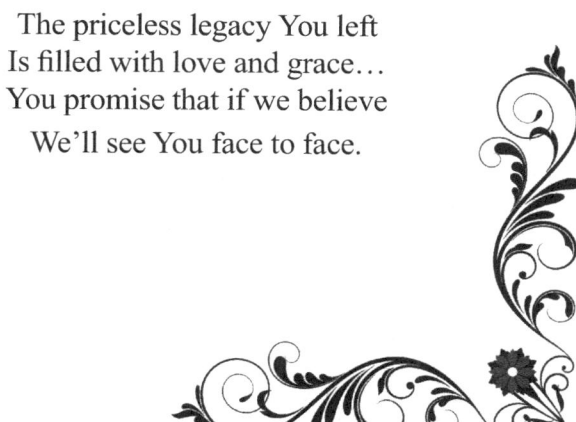

Fatherly Love

Our Father flinched as they hammered each nail,
But He had to endure His Son's cry.
He planned that Christ's blood would redeem us…
The reason Christ came was to die.

With each blow, our sins were heaped on Him;
Their weight caused unbearable pain.
Yet He never complained for one moment…
The Perfect Lamb had to be slain.

For unless we had a Redeemer,
Heaven's gate would forever be closed…
But thanks to God's love and forgiveness,
It opened the morning Christ rose.

Frances Gregory Pasch

Precious, Priceless Prize

How can we ever thank You
For dying in our place!
You suffered pain and anguish…
The ultimate disgrace.

You opened not Your mouth to cry,
Despite the stress and strain.
You bore our sins and all their weight,
Yet never did complain.

They tortured You and beat You,
Placed thorns upon Your head,
Drove nails into Your hands and feet
And mocked You as You bled.

But little did they know, O Lord,
That soon You would arise
And free us from the sting of death,
A precious, priceless prize.

Made in USA - Kendallville, IN
1203678_9798559528007